For Frances Gilbert—much!

—T.S.

For Sara and Sonya

—D.M.

Visit us on the Web! rhcbooks.com

Educators and librarians, for a variety of teaching tools, visit us at RHTeachersLibrarians.com

Library of Congress Cataloging-in-Publication Data
Names: Sauer, Tammi, author. | Mottram, Dave, illustrator.
Title: Wordy Birdy meets Mr. Cougarpants / by Tammi Sauer ; illustrated by Dave Mottram.
Description: First edition. | New York : Doubleday, [2019]
Summary: "When Wordy Birdy and her friends go on a camping trip, they get an unexpected visit from
Mr. Cougarpants. Can Wordy Birdy talk herself out of becoming dinner?" —Provided by publisher.
Identifiers: LCCN 2018001394 (print) | LCCN 2018008833 (ebook)
ISBN 978-1-5247-1933-3 (hc) | ISBN 978-1-5247-1931-9 (glb) | ISBN 978-1-5247-1936-4 (ebk)
Subjects: | CYAC: Camping—Fiction. | Birds—Fiction. | Puma—Fiction. | Animals—Fiction. | Conversation—Fiction.
Classification: LCC PZ7.S2502 Wok 2019 (print) | LCC PZ7.S2502 (ebook) | DDC [E]—dc23

Book design by Nicole de las Heras

MANUFACTURED IN CHINA
10 9 8 7 6 5 4 3 2 1
First Edition

WORDY BiRDY
MEETS MR. COUGARPANTS

Written by Tammi Sauer   Illustrated by Dave Mottram

Doubleday Books for Young Readers

Wordy Birdy is a little chatty.

Okay, fine. Wordy Birdy is super chatty. She talks all day long. Even when she shouldn't.

One day, Wordy Birdy goes camping with her friends.
Of course, she has *lots* to say.

Squirrel goes to bed.
Rabbit goes to bed.
Raccoon goes to bed.
Does Wordy Birdy go to bed?

At last, Wordy Birdy finishes snacking.
Then Rabbit yawns.

Good night, everybody.

Rabbit shuts his eyes.
Raccoon shuts his eyes.
Squirrel shuts his eyes.
Does Wordy Birdy shut her eyes?

At last, Wordy Birdy finishes wishing.

I have an idea. Let's play the quiet game.

Raccoon gets quiet.
Squirrel gets quiet.
Rabbit gets quiet.
Does Wordy Birdy get quiet when a big,
hungry cougar wants to gobble them all up?

Mr. Cougarpants can't take this one more minute.
He turns and flees into the deep, deep, *peaceful* woods.

Wordy Birdy is still chatty.
Sometimes she's *too* chatty.

But her friends wouldn't want her any other way.